DRIPPING WET

COME ON IN, THE WATER'S WARM.

MIKA LANE

HEADLANDS PUBLISHING

COPYRIGHT

Like deals and other cool stuff?
Sign up for my newsletter!

GET A FREE STORY!

Get a free short story!

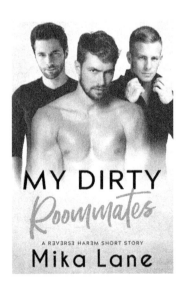

Join my Insider Group

Exclusive access to private release specials, giveaways, the opportunity to receive advance reader copies (ARCs), and other random musings.

NOTE TO READERS

HELLO MY ROMANCE LOVERS! I'M SO GLAD YOU'RE HERE to check out Aspen's story in *Dripping Wet*, from the **Filthy Dirty Summer** collection, and how she goes on one wild ride with her gorgeous men, Teague, Luke, and Brant. Get ready for a story of forbidden, naughty, and redemptive love with sexy fun that will leave you wanting more.

SCREEEEECHHHHHH.

Oh hell no.

There is little worse than nails on a chalkboard, other than the sound of the car you weren't supposed to be driving colliding with a mailbox. That high-pitched, ear-splitting squeal of metal on metal is without a doubt worse, particularly when your shitty driving skills are the cause of it.

From where I sat, in the driver's seat, the passenger side mirror provided a perfect view of where the nasty sound had originated.

I put the car in *reverse* and gave it a little gas, as if that might undo my mistake.

Screeeechhhhhh.

Not helping.

I wasn't sure how to move the car off the faux-rustic post, designed to fit with the house it collected mail for —one of those old-fashioned mailbox jobs with the flag to let you know whether or not you'd gotten mail.

Did weekend homes really get mail? Or was this another façade, one of many that my famous and rich fashion designer boss cultivated with excellence?

Ready to kill some*one* or some*thing*, I exited the car with the intention of assessing the damage I'd caused. But I stopped before I'd rounded the trunk. I didn't have the balls to see exactly what I'd done, at least not at that moment. But I'd have to deal with it at some point, because I was there, in part, to pick up the freaking mail.

And while this was a bad situation all around, the worst of it was that the car was my boss's, a shiny white BMW, also representative of the perfect life she had, or at least made the world think she had.

So no, I didn't have permission to drive her car.

I'd messed up. Big time.

I looked up the long, gravel driveway leading to Lake LaRenne's massive Southampton 'weekend house' as she called it, and then back at her pretty car.

The one I wasn't supposed to drive.

Car and mailbox damage aside, it was an image of affluent perfection. An oversized house on the beach, covered in weathered shingles to make it look a little rustic and, well, beachy, could have nothing other than a luxury car in its drive. No, a Honda Civic, like my parents drove back in Iowa, would have been ridiculously out of place.

I never should have taken her car. I knew that from the moment I drove out of her Manhattan garage, where her monthly parking spot lease cost as much as my monthly rent.

But for fuck's sake, the woman was over in France or Italy chasing Eurodick like she did several times a year when she traveled abroad for 'meetings' or some bullshit.

I knew her latest conquest was a chiseled male model at least twenty years her junior because he'd sent a dickpic—to *me*.

Yeah, the dumbass pretty boy had confused her phone number with mine, which she loved to give out so all the world knew she was important enough to have an assistant. Because of that, I occasionally got her calls or texts.

But the dickpic had been a first. Particularly since it was of an uncircumcised penis. Thus, the term, Eurodick.

I grabbed my duffel from the BMW's front seat, slammed the car door, and pressed *lock* on the key fob. Like anyone was going to try and steal a car stuck to a mailbox post anyway.

As I trudged toward the house on the uneven gravel in my platforms, the sea air whipped hair around my face. While for a moment I enjoyed the scent of the ocean, I remembered I'd just washed my hair that morning and did not want it turning into a ball of frizz. I pulled my hoodie up and followed the crunchy path to the front door, let myself in, and turned off the house alarm before it could start blaring.

The ninety-five-ish mile drive from Manhattan hadn't been too bad. I mean, of course there was the usual New York and Long Island traffic, but I'd had the music cranked, the sunroof open, and even if I were sitting in traffic, at least I was doing it in a sweet ride. I'd never driven a BMW.

Shit, I'd never even *been* in one.

But a nice car and cool tunes can only distract a person for so long when sitting in bumper-to-bumper New York traffic. So naturally, the very thing I was hoping to forget popped up in my thoughts like a bad penny—my recent ex. I wasn't so bent out of shape that he'd dumped my ass—which he had—but because he'd had the nerve to tell me I never took chances. Played it too safe. Didn't have what it took to take risks.

I was boring.

Well, he didn't say that last bit, but I was pretty sure that's what he was getting at.

And, look at me now.

I'd just driven my boss's car out to the Hamptons on a summer weekend, and now was in her freaking insane beach house.

Suck on that, motherfucker.

A little car accident notwithstanding.

I stood in the doorway of Lake's house, taking it all in. As expected, it was a perfectly-designed blend of rustic-but-not-too-rustic chic, with huge abstract paint-ings on the wall providing a dizzying contrast to the splintery wood planks of the foyer floor, and long bench that looked like it had been lifted from an old church.

I walked farther into the house, marveling that someone could own something like this and hardly ever use it. And, apparently, she now wanted to get rid of it. That's why she'd sent me here. I was supposed to take the Hampton Jitney weekend bus to not only pick up the mail and a couple other things, but to also make sure everything was in tip-top shape for the real estate agent's private showings scheduled for tomorrow and Sunday.

Why hadn't I just taken the damn bus?

Oh right. It was because I *was* someone who took chances. I *didn't* play it safe. I had what it took to take risks.

I was *not* boring.

Look where that had gotten me.

I wandered through the living room with its giant, white, overstuffed sofas and loveseats, stacks of strate-gically-placed coffee table books, and high-end scented candles I recognized from the ones she often burned in the office. I was tempted to plop onto one of those sofas and put my feet up, but after what I'd done to the BMW, I was going to be very careful about what I touched.

Although when she found out what I'd done to the car, I'd probably be fired, anyway. So, I just tossed my hoodie onto a chair, pretending for a moment that I actually lived there.

I opened a couple windows to air the place out. No one had been there in so long it had gotten musty.

And as I did, I heard voices. Male voices.

I knew the Hamptons were generally safe, given that they were the summer playground for the New York wealthy, but I also knew no one was expected there at the house except me.

I grabbed my cell phone and crept toward the back

of the house, following the noise. As I did, it got louder, like shouting-louder.

"Move it fucker!" a male voice shouted.

Oh my god.

I dialed 9-1-1 and kept my finger on the *send* button, ready to alert the authorities.

The shouting continued, followed by a loud crash.

Thank god I'd come along when I had, but when I spotted the source of the voices—three men—I saw they weren't your everyday intruders. Rather, they looked like models from a Ralph Lauren catalogue.

But who knew? Maybe that's what burglars looked like in this preppy part of the world.

I pushed open a kitchen window just far enough to shout, finger still on the 9-1-1 *send* button. "Hey. What's going on here?" I hollered in my best badass voice.

The noise came to an immediate stop, and when I stuck my head out the window farther, I saw various backyard-tending sorts of equipment.

Were they stealing this stuff? Who in the Hamptons steals hedge clippers?

The three guys whipped around to face me, clearly as surprised to see me as I was them.

"Well?" I demanded.

"Oh. Hey," one said, scraping his hair off his forehead with one hand and giving me a wave with the other.

Holy shit, he was gorgeous. I mean, there were plenty of good-looking guys in Manhattan, but I'd never seen the likes of this.

Focus, idiot.

"Are… are you supposed to be here?" I asked, keeping my voice low and menacing.

Unbothered, they looked at each other and shrugged.

"Yeah," one said, picking up a pool skimmer. "I'm cleaning the pool and Brant here is trimming the bushes."

Brant stepped forward. "Well, I *will* be trimming the bushes as soon as I chase off the raccoons nesting in there. Little bastards."

I turned to the guy who'd said hello. "What about you? What are you doing here?" I asked.

With his hands on his hips, he smiled and looked down at his feet for a moment, then looked back at me with a swagger no doubt designed to knock me off my feet.

Try again, mister.

"I'm just along for the ride with my buddies. You know, helping them out," he said with a cocky, lopsided grin. "Someone's gotta supervise these losers."

That earned him a slap on the back of the head with the long-handled pool skimmer.

"Fuck off, dude," he said, rubbing his head and laughing.

Okay. I knew his type.

I slipped my cell phone into the pocket of my dress, but frowned in an effort to maintain my authority. "Lake didn't tell me anyone would be here," I snapped.

Mister Swagger took a couple steps toward the house. "We come every Friday. But we weren't told *you* would be here. So who are you?"

Really? He wanted to play like that?

I pulled the kitchen window shut and walked over to the sliding glass door off a gigantic, tiled dining room. It overlooked a covered patio appointed with what looked to be very expensive teak furnishings, a sparkling swimming pool, and the ocean beyond.

Holy shit. No wonder she had to hire people to maintain all this. And she wanted to sell it? The woman was crazy.

I stepped out onto the patio and stretched to my full height. It wasn't lost on me that the guys were eyeing me up and down, staring at my platform sandals and my short and swingy summer dress. "I'm Lake's assistant, Aspen. Why didn't I see your cars out front?"

Brant lowered his sunglasses and gestured toward the side of the property. "The service entrance is over there. That's where we always park."

Service entrance? What planet had I just landed on?

The cocky one approached me with an outstretched hand. "I'm Teague," he said with a devilish smile. "That's Brant with the backward cap. And mister man-bun over there is Luke."

Now that I could see the totality of them, I was glad I hadn't been a bigger bitch. Dark suntans and physiques sculpted by hard work were weaknesses of mine.

Brant and Luke, continuing to drip with sweat even during my interrogation, were shirtless. Their cargo shorts hung well below their waists. Brant's exposed the top of his boxers, and Luke's revealed some dark hair that disappeared beneath his waistband—

Down girl.

Teague, who clearly thought his shit didn't stink, was the only one not sweating. A T-shirt stretched across his chest and around his biceps and now I knew Lake was *really* crazy for giving up her house. She preferred Eurodick to *this*?

"How long have you worked for Miss LaRenne?" Luke asked politely, hiking up his shorts after he'd seen me staring.

Long enough for her to realize my design talent and steal my ideas, adding to her already-massive fashion empire.

Well, I wasn't completely certain she was stealing my ideas. But I had a strong suspicion, after her latest collection had come out eerily similar to some of the drawings I'd done for her.

Drawings of mine that she patiently explained needed a lot more work before they'd be viable design options.

Seemed they were viable enough for her to steal, though.

"I've been her assistant for about six months. I was chosen out of hundreds of recent fashion design gradu-ates," I said proudly.

Ugh. Why was I telling these guys this? I was sure they couldn't give a shit about the latest chick to waltz into town from the city and act like she owned the place.

To prove I wasn't one of those, I backpedaled a little. "Hey, sorry I grilled you guys. I was worried you were, you know, burglars or something."

Luke waved his hand like it was nothing. "We surprise people all the time. They forget they scheduled us, or arrive, like you did, when we're in the middle of our work. No harm done."

Teague rolled his shoulders back and puffed out his chest. Because, of course. "That's true, *but* we're not usually confronted by someone as attractive as you."

I looked at him a minute to see if he was pulling my leg, and when the sincere expression remained on his face, I doubled over, fake-laughing.

What the hell else could I do? One of the most beautiful men I'd ever seen had just paid me a compliment. He might have been blowing smoke up my ass, but on some level it still felt nice, especially after the ex left me feeling so… lacking.

"That's very nice of you to say, Teague," I said, regaining my footing. "So guys, there are some private open houses for this place tomorrow and Sunday. So please do your best and make the grounds beautiful. It will make my boss very happy."

Brant started throwing his tools into a wheelbarrow and wiped the sweat from his eyes. "Miss LaRenne is selling? Are you kidding? This is one of the best properties in town."

I nodded and rolled my eyes in agreement. "Can you believe it? I think she wants to get a place in the south of France. Figures she won't be out here often enough anymore."

"Interesting. We usually know when properties are going on the market," he said, looking at his buddies.

Teague thoughtfully scratched his chin. "Yeah. Interesting."

I wasn't sure what was so interesting about a house going up for sale, but I didn't want to keep these guys from their work.

I had some things to do, myself.

"Well then maybe one of you guys should buy it," I said, laughing. I pulled the door closed, locking myself inside.

They waved and got back to what they were doing, Luke fiddling with the pool, Brant using some motorized thing to trim the bushes, and Teague standing there, staring back at the house.

———

2

MY PHONE BUZZED AND I LOOKED DOWN TO SEE IT WAS none other than Lake LaRenne herself.

"Hi, Lake," I said, as if I'd not just crashed her BMW.

"Aspen! Are you at the house? How was the Jitney?" she sang.

There was some sort of racket in the background. Like a squeaking bed.

Ew.

"Um, yeah, it was great. Yup. All is well. Just got here a bit ago. I'm opening some windows to let fresh air in. The pool guy and landscaper are out back."

There was a rustle of fabric and the sound of a slap.

"Eek!" she said. "Sorry, Aspen. I am just so damned busy here. Thank you for checking on the house for me. Don't forget my mail and to grab the laptop I left on the kitchen counter. Make yourself at home tonight in the guest bedroom but please be sure to wash the sheets before you catch the 8am bus back to the city. '*Kay*?"

Was she serious? She wanted me to get up, do laundry, and take the first bus home? She was freaking crazy.

Of course, I was crazy to have taken her car. But I'd deal with that later.

"Aspen? Are you still there?" she asked, another slap and another *eek* following.

God, she was rude. I mean, I knew she talked to me over the phone when she was on the toilet taking a pee and stuff, but while Eurodick was slapping her ass?

Just no.

I was staying in her goddamn house as long as I felt like it. Well, I'd be back at work on Monday, but still.

And the ex said I never took risks?

Ha.

"Sounds good, Lake, just a little hard to hear you over long distance, ya know?" I lied while poking through her freezer and helping myself to some fancy designer ice cream. That was somehow fat-free.

"Great, Aspen, and feel free to help yourself to anything in the kitchen, okay?"

I shoveled a spoonful of the ice cream in my mouth. "Thanks. Sounds good."

"Okay. *A bientot*!" she sang. "I'm learning French," she giggled, and was gone.

Just as I was reading the side of the ice cream carton to try and figure out how something so good could be fat-free, there was a rap on the back door.

I slid it open a few inches.

"Hey, we're leaving now. Just wanted to let you know," Luke said, pulling out his man bun and shaking the sweat out of his hair.

And when he did, I caught his scent, which I would have expected to be gross from working in the hot sun, but was actually a delicious mix of some sort of masculine soap and the slightest whiff of body odor. It was so appealing, I had to stuff my hands in my pockets to keep from removing the small twig stuck in his hair.

Cripes. Maybe I should invite him in for... water or something?

"Oh, okay," I said, wiping a drop of ice cream from the front of my dress, "you thirsty?"

He pointed toward what he'd called the 'service entrance.' "We have a cooler in the truck. Thanks though. You heading out soon?" he asked.

I nodded. "Yup. Back to the city," I said, cheerfully.

They didn't need to know my plans.

They took off across the lawn, waving over their shoulders.

Alone at last.

Having devoured the ice cream, I grabbed a big glass of water and wandered onto the patio, which now not only smelled of the ocean air, but also the just-cut greenery of Lake's yard. What I wouldn't do to bottle that.

Guess that's why people had beach houses.

After kicking off my platforms, I circled the pool, dipping a toe to test the temperature.

Perfection.

Looking around to make sure I had total privacy, I slipped my dress off over my head, dropped my bra to the ground, and dove in, just wearing my panties.

Pure heaven.

I did a couple mini-laps, then moved to the center of the pool, where I treaded water for a while. I had no access to a swimming pool in Manhattan, so this was a treat of massive proportion.

Floating on my back, I watched the water bead up on my stomach and breasts. The warm sun and the sound of the ocean were mesmerizing, and I realized I was tired. Well, I was always tired. I found life in Manhattan to be exhausting. All the people, the long hours one was expected to work, and the high cost of just about everything left me in a near-constant state of anxiety.

So, I got out of the pool, lay down on the warm concrete deck just next to it, and bunched up my dress to use as a little pillow.

I don't know how long I'd been snoozing before I was startled awake. For a split second, I looked up at the blue sky and my gorgeous surroundings and wasn't sure where I was.

But when my head did clear and familiar voices grew closer, I panicked, grabbing my dress and wrestling it over my head. In the struggle to make myself decent, I yanked it hard. Too hard. It responded with a long *riiiip* down the side seam, followed by my forgotten cell phone slipping from its pocket.

Into the pool.

Yay, me.

Tossing the dress aside, I dove back into the pool after my phone, grabbing it just before it hit bottom. When I surfaced, I shook it, as if that would do anything, and realized the voices were of the guys who'd been there earlier.

What the hell were they doing back? Did they forget something?

I silently set my phone on the pool deck and lowered myself back into the water under the pool's edge, in the hope that if they were just passing through, they might not notice me.

Yeah, right.

From the direction of the service entrance, the guys came into view, just as hot and handsome as they had been earlier in the day, but this time wearing big smiles and carrying a small cooler.

No way. Were they here for a swim? To help themselves to Lake's pool?

Assholes.

Although, I supposed I wasn't much better, helping myself to Lake's car. *And* pool.

They were going to notice me sooner or later, so I decided to outflank them. "Hey," I shouted, "you guys aren't supposed to be here."

Startled, they followed my voice until they spotted me.

"Oh. Look who it is," Teague said, clearly undeterred, ripping off his shirt and removing his cargo shorts to reveal blue swim trunks.

He smiled and jogged over to the pool. "Holy shit, guys. Aspen isn't wearing anything. What happened, forget your bathing suit?" He laughed, diving in.

No, no, no. This was not supposed to happen.

I cowered in a corner of the pool, legs drawn up out

of modesty, and started to wave my arm like shooing away a fly. "Get out. You're not allowed in here," I insisted.

But he just swam to the middle of the pool without a care in the world, treading water in the same spot I had earlier. He tilted his wet, chiseled face up to the blue sky and closed his eyes. How could someone so annoying be so handsome?

"Gorgeous day. Freaking gorgeous, isn't it?" He flipped onto his back and with a little flutter of his hands, began to float.

I looked over at Brant and Luke, who seemed like they were at least considering my demand that they hit the road.

"Hey, Teague, we should probably go—" Brant started to say.

But Luke cut him off. "Why is your phone sitting in a puddle of water?" he asked, hustling around the edge of the pool to where I'd left it, politely pretending I wasn't nearly naked by looking everywhere but in my direction.

He picked it up and gave it a little shake. "Oh shit. Phone in the pool," he said.

Still balled up in the corner, I nodded. "Yup."

He turned it upside down and then back up. "I may be able to fix it," he said.

"Nah, Luke, she said we have to leave. We'd better get out of here," Teague chanted before he dove under the water and did a handstand.

Dick.

Brant joined Luke in checking over my waterlogged

phone. "Hey, how 'bout we give it a shot?" he asked. "Is there any rice in the kitchen?"

I shrugged, trying to figure out how I could cover myself with a torn dress that was clear across the pool. "You can go check if you want."

They nodded at each other and headed for the house.

Teague surfaced, a little closer to me than I would have liked. "You know, I'm all about skinny dipping too. In fact, I could skinny dip right now." He made like he was about to remove his swim trunks.

"No!" I yelled. "Would you please go get me a towel so I can get out of the pool without exposing myself? Please?"

He rolled his eyes and swam to the edge where he hoisted himself out of the water and onto the deck in one smooth movement. The water beaded up on his back, glistening in the sun and highlighting the graceful swell of the muscles in his back.

He might be a smart ass but he sure was a good looking one.

He grabbed a towel off a lounge chair and turned to face me, his handsome brow all the more prominent with his hair slicked off his face. As he walked toward me, he ran his fingers through it, shaking it out, his gaze locked with mine.

And yes, he wore that smirky little half-smile that both irritated the shit out of me, and tickled my core at the same time.

What the fuck?

"Here," he said, holding the towel up like a big

curtain over by the pool's steps. "I'll hold this and close my eyes while you climb out."

Well. A gentleman after all.

I dog paddled across the pool so as not to expose myself, and with a glance around to make sure no one was looking, I bounded up the steps as fast as the water would let me, and leapt for the towel.

But I wasn't fast enough.

In a lightning-fast move, Teague pulled the towel away from me and turned to stare, taking in my panty-clad, dripping wet body.

"You asshole," I screamed, and lunged for the towel with a ferocity that made his eyes widen through his laughter.

"Jesus, take it," he said, giving up and tossing it toward me while wisely taking two steps back.

I quickly wrapped myself and marched over to the cooler the guys had brought. I pulled out a can of Bud, which I chucked with all my might in Teague's direction. The first one skimmed his shoulder before it landed in the bushes.

"Hey, hey, that's our beer," he hollered.

I grabbed the next can and threw it, this time missing him completely but hitting the deck, where it exploded its fizzy contents all over the concrete.

He bent to pick it up as if he could salvage a few sips, when I took aim one last time and hit him right in the chest.

"Ow, shit," he yelled, stumbling forward and placing a hand on the spot where I'd beaned him.

My work was done.

There were three beers left in the cooler, so I grabbed one and popped the top on it, taking a nice, long swig.

I hadn't had a beer in ages.

Brant and Luke appeared in the doorway at the commotion.

Fuck 'em all.

"Ugh, guys, what's going on?" Brant asked, looking at the beer cans strewn over the backyard, Teague rubbing the store spot on his chest.

What a baby.

"Well," I said after lifting my beer in salute to the guys, "Teague thought he was entitled to a look at me getting out of the pool. I got a little... pissed."

Luke looked around, his eyes wide. "Guess so."

I walked around to the side of the pool and retrieved my torn dress. "Any word on my phone, guys?"

Brant looked up from the mess I'd made. "Oh. Yeah. It's sitting in the rice we found in the cupboard. Time will tell if it's gonna work. You never know."

"But it's worth trying," Luke added.

Shit. First Lake's car. Now my phone. And I couldn't get rid of these pesty guys.

"What? Did you call us pesty?" Teague asked.

Oops. Had I said that out loud?

"Whatever," I mumbled, collapsing onto a lounge chair, clutching the towel around me in one hand and my ruined dress in the other.

"Um, another thing, Aspen," Luke said cautiously, "what's up with that car out front? The one that's smashed into the mailbox?"

All right. That was it. I'd had enough.

I buried my face in my hands and moaned. Loudly. "That's my boss's car. Which I was not supposed to be driving."

"Oh shit, you crashed your boss's car?" Brant asked.

I looked up at him and nodded slowly. "I'm fucked. Plain and simple, I'm fucked. She thinks I took the Jitney here and am returning on it at 8am tomorrow. After I launder the sheets I've slept on, of course."

I laughed weakly and it wasn't until a pain shot through my jaw that I realized I'd been clenching, actually, grinding my teeth.

What a mess.

"We… we could take a look at it for you," he said.

I looked up at him through squinted eyes. A headache was circling my head like a hungry vulture. "You can?" I croaked.

I wanted them out of there, but I wasn't an idiot.

"Where're the keys?" he asked.

I gestured toward the house as Luke and Brant trotted off to their next task.

And who joined me by taking a seat at the end of my lounge chair but Teague. He put a hand on my calf and patted me gently. "Sorry I teased you with the towel, Aspen. I didn't realize you were that close to the edge, ready to lose your shit."

Close to the edge. Ready to lose my shit.

Well put.

I sighed. "It's all right. I know you were just playing around. Although I'm still not happy you got to see me in my panties." I tried to sound pissed, but couldn't suppress the giggle that escaped.

"There ya go," he said. "Finding the humor. I like that. Don't worry, Aspen, we can help you out of this mess. We know everyone here in town and most everything that goes on. You've stumbled into the right guys."

I shrugged, picking at what was left of last month's manicure. Lake might have been providing me a great job opportunity, despite her stealing my designs, but she paid shit. The only reason I had a manicure was that my parents had sent me money for my birthday.

"C'mon, Aspen," Teague said, moving to the head of my lounger and pulling me to him with an arm around my shoulders.

I let my head rest on him. Why the hell not?

"I will say," he said quietly, "you looked pretty fucking awesome standing there, all shiny and wet, in those clingy, sheer panties."

I peeked up at him, preparing to give him a major stink-eye, but before I could, something came over me.

And I pressed my lips to his.

I really did.

It made no sense. But I didn't care.

I figured that in light of an otherwise shit day, the universe owed me something, even if it were just a quick kiss with a handsome man.

It was becoming apparent to me, never a particularly fast learner, that taking risks was not without its price. But some things were just worth it.

3

"JESUS, GUYS. GET A ROOM."

I jerked away from Teague's surprisingly soft lips and found Luke and Brant standing there, watching.

"Oh, hey," I said, bolting to my feet and pulling the towel tighter.

Teague leaned back on the lounge chair wearing his usual shit-eating grin. "Leave it to you fuckers to cock-block me."

Brant rolled his eyes. "If you two are done sucking face, we can talk about the car. We have someone on their way over to get it. Lucky for you, Aspen, we see a lot of BMWs here in Southampton, and my cousin owns his own body shop. He should be able to slot you in tomorrow morning. If he's in a really good mood and I buy him a nice bottle of scotch, he might even work on Sunday to get it finished so you can be back in the city for work Monday."

"Oh my god!" I squealed, running to throw my arms around him while gripping my towel in modesty. "I don't know how I will repay you for this. You have no idea how you are saving my ass."

Good news and bad. The car was being repaired… but I'd have to pay for it. I started mental calculations of how much open credit I had.

The headache started circling again.

"I'll tell ya something, Aspen. If your boss had called the shop, they would have put her off till next week," he added. "But we hooked you up."

Things were working out in my favor.

"Thank you again. It sure helps to know the locals, I guess. Now all I have to do is get my phone up and running, and I'll be in great shape."

I followed Luke around the pool, where he was picking up the beer cans I'd thrown. "What would be great, Aspen, was if you went and got dressed, and came to happy hour with us," he said.

Teague looked at his watch and jumped to his feet. "Party time!" he sang, pulling his cargo shorts back on over his now-dry bathing suit.

Luke looked longingly at the pool. "Damn, I didn't even get a swim in."

"What were you guys doing back here, anyway? Besides trespassing, that is."

"We thought you'd be gone. To be honest, we swim here all the time," Brant said.

Holy crap. If Lake knew that, her head would freaking explode. But she wasn't going to find out from me.

"You don't have anywhere else to swim?" I asked.

Brant and Luke looked over at Teague.

"My dad's house here has a pool, but my grandparents spend most of their summer there. So, sure we swim there, but sometimes it's fun to just chill someplace away from them," he said.

Luke laughed. "His grandmother is awesome, but she's always asking us to buy her wine behind his grandfather's back. It gets awkward."

"Your dad has a house here, Teague?" I asked.

He nodded, still not looking at me. "Yeah. I grew up spending summers here, hanging out with these losers."

"Teague lives in LA. His old man is some film muckety-muck," Luke said. "In fact, at the end of this summer, we're thinking about driving cross-country, then starting a landscaping business in LA."

So these guys weren't just party boys. They had plans.

Brant clapped his hands behind me, scaring the shit out of me. "C'mon. Go get dressed. We have cheap beers to drink."

I grabbed my duffel from the foyer and after a quick check on my phone, now submerged in rice, I ran upstairs. Lake had told me to stay in the room overlooking the garage because it was her natural inclination to stick me in the shittiest part of the house. But when I passed what looked to be the primary bedroom, with its views of the lovely backyard and the ocean beyond, I dropped my bag there.

Fuck it. I was taking the good room.

I took a quick rinse, twisted my hair up into a bun, and pulled on the only other dress I'd packed. Stepping into my platforms, I twirled in front of the huge mirror in the corner of the room, and had to admit that my short, ruffled dress was just right for a night out in a beach town. I made sure to put on my cutest panties just in case the wind blew hard, and walked down the stairs with a little bounce in my step.

The guys looked up when my platforms clomped onto the patio.

"Let's get this party started!" I hollered.

Nobody moved.

"Oh my god. Is something wrong? Is it the car? *What?*" I demanded, looking from one to the other.

"Um, well, wow," Brant said after a moment. "You look… amazing."

What? These guys were crazy, and if they thought they were getting into my panties, they had another think coming.

I may have kissed Teague, but that was a fluke. It wouldn't happen again.

At least that's what I told myself as I followed them to the service entrance on the side of the house, straight to Luke's Jeep Wrangler.

Teague held the front passenger door for me, and I gratefully snagged the shotgun seat.

The engine rumbled under us as it came to life. "So. What does everyone think of having the top open tonight?" Luke yelled over the racket.

All eyes turned in my direction. "Sure. It's a beautiful summer night. Let's do it," I said, pulling my hair out of its bun.

A few minutes later, we were on our way to town, music blasting and salt air blowing in our faces. In spite of the crap day I'd had, I hadn't felt so happy and care-free since... I didn't know when. I certainly never had this feeling in New York City. As much as it was the land of opportunity, the frenetic pace was a weight that always felt an inch away from squashing me to nothing, sending me back to the podunk town in Iowa I'd worked so hard to get away from.

But with the sea in the air, and three hot new friends, I had all a girl could ask for on a pretty summer evening.

Right?

The bouncing of the Jeep meant I had to hold on tight, and when I reached to grab something, anything with my left hand, my fingers brushed Luke's. He continued to look ahead, concentrating on the summer resort traffic, but his hand didn't move away from mine. In fact, two of his fingers intertwined with mine and his thumb stroked the bony part of my wrist. While he was touching not much more than a couple square inches of my skin, I tingled all over, my senses height-ening as if in preparation for more. I'd just met this guy —and his buddies—but there was something about them. Like they were the missing puzzle piece that you find on the floor under your chair after looking all over the place.

But that was silly. Right?

After parking, we noisily crunched over the parking lot that was, according to the guys, made of crushed oyster shells. Teague stopped us before we got to the door.

"Okay. Aspen. Heads up. This is a divey little bar, as

you are about to see. But it's also the coolest bar in the Hamptons. Celebrities come here all the time."

If it was good enough for a celebrity, it was good enough for me.

We entered the dim space, and while it took a moment for my eyes to adjust to the lack of light, a hand fell on the small of my back. I turned to find Brant smiling down on me. My pulse jumped to full speed, and by the time we reached the bar, I was nearly breathless. I slid onto the stool Teague pulled out for me, grinning like a freaking idiot.

Luke appeared at my side holding a pitcher of beer and four plastic cups. He poured for me first, then filled the others.

He raised his cup. "To summer," he said, and then looked directly at me. "And to beautiful women who swim naked. Or nearly naked."

A blast of warmth heated my face. "Did... all you guys see me or something?"

A guilty look passed over Brant's face. "Of course we did. You think we barge in on someone's backyard without checking first to make sure no one's there?"

Teague stifled a laugh behind his beer cup. "They wanted to leave. I convinced them you wouldn't care if we crashed."

The man was infuriating.

"So... when you pretended to be surprised to see me, that was just an act?" Of course, I already knew the answer.

And they confirmed it, smiling and nodding.

Well for fuck's sake.

"Ok. Fine," I said, holding my head up. "That means I get to see you guys skinny dipping. It's only fair."

They looked at each other and shrugged, and I realized they couldn't give a shit if I saw them butt-naked.

So much for that.

I slipped off my stool and set my beer on the bar. "I'm going to pee."

I wound my way through the bar's growing crowd, amused that a place with splintered floors, smelling of stale beer, and fisherman's nets hanging from the eaves could be considered a 'celebrity hangout.' But I did pass by a booth in a dark corner where I could swear I saw Leonardo DiCaprio smiling and talking with friends…

Guess everyone loves a dive bar every now and then.

I walked down the steep stairs to the bar's basement, where the restrooms were tucked away, and tiptoed down a narrow hallway dodging beer kegs. I got to the ladies', and pulling the door closed, took care of business.

But when I was washing my hands, someone startled the shit out of me by appearing right behind me in the sink mirror.

"Oh my god. You almost gave me a heart attack," I said, turning to face Luke. Must have wandered into the wrong restroom.

Or not.

Shit, he was tall. Even with my platforms on, I had to look up at him. And now that we were close, closer than we'd been, I could see a cute little scar on his chin.

I pressed my finger to it. "That from a childhood bike wreck?"

He grabbed my hand and pulled it to his lips. "See. I knew you were a normal person who could relate to the stupid things we do as kids."

I could also relate to the stupid things we did as adults, but my mouth was too dry to say so.

He stepped closer, closing the space between us. The only thing behind me was the bathroom sink. I couldn't go anywhere.

Not that I wanted to.

"Um, ugh, Luke—"

I couldn't spit out one coherent sentence. But I didn't need to. Luke took up the slack.

"Aspen, I couldn't resist following you down here. I know that's creepy stalker behavior, but I had to have a moment alone with you."

He ran his fingers through my hair, a tangled mess from the Jeep.

"You're the ideal summer girl, Aspen, with your little dress, wild hair, and sunburned shoulders. You know what you do to me?"

"I, well, um—"

And because I couldn't form a damn sentence, his lips landed on mine while his giant hands gripped my waist, nearly encircling them, pulling me closer. With my mouth pressed to his, I wildly looked around the ladies' room to see if there was anyone else around, but it seemed we had the place to ourselves. At least for the moment.

Even through his firm kiss, his lips were soft and exploring, and so much better than my ex's.

What had I been thinking with that jerk?

Satisfied we had the place to ourselves, I let my eyes fall closed, permitting me to sink into Luke's hard body. Pressed against me, there was no doubt a bulge was forming in his pants, which was a nice match to the wet spot now collecting on my panties.

And it didn't go unnoticed by Luke. He slipped a hand under my short dress, running a finger along the elastic leg of my panties until he reached the inner crease of my thigh. He moved his finger back and forth there for a moment, so close to my core, and yet so far that I tried to maneuver myself into his touch.

I wanted him to know how wet he was getting me.

Jesus, who *was* I?

With a fistful of my hair, he turned my head to the side and ran his lips along the shell of my ear. "Fuck, baby, you know how much I like a smooth pussy?" he murmured, running his finger over my shaved lips without dipping between them.

A shiver plowed through me as he teased my flesh. I decided to take action. What the hell. I'd never be back here. I'd never see these guys again.

"Do you want to show me how much you like my shaved pussy, Luke?" I said quietly.

He promptly released my hair. "Fuck yeah," he growled.

I took his hand and led him to the last stall in the ladies' room, and not a moment too soon. A couple giggling girls flew in, followed by the click of lipstick tubes opening and closing.

Not to mention dishing. "Holy shit. Did you see those three guys up there at the bar? And how about the tall one with the man bun. What I wouldn't do to suck his dick."

"Seriously." The other one sighed. "I'd even let him take my ass, he's so hot."

I clamped my hand over my mouth, pressed up against Luke in the small bathroom stall, and tried not to laugh. He, on the other hand, rolled his eyes and shook his head.

"Is that what it's like for you here? All summer, girls are just throwing themselves at you?" I whispered.

"No. No it is not."

Bullshit.

The gigglers left, and I slipped my panties down to my ankles and stepped out of them, hanging them on the bathroom door hook. Then, I lifted a leg to place my foot on the toilet seat, and raised my dress just enough to give Luke a little show.

"Goddamn. That's what I'm talking about," he said, bending to get closer.

4

LUKE RAN ONE SWIPE OF HIS TONGUE THROUGH MY PUSSY lips when someone pounded on the bathroom door.

"Ugh," he groaned. "Who the fuck is that?"

As if hearing a loud, annoyed male in a ladies' room happened every day.

"Luke, you fucker, I knew you were in there," Teague said, rapping his knuckles on the flimsy stall door. "'C'-mon. I just got us invited to a party. Put your dick back in your pants. Let's go."

I quickly rearranged myself by putting my foot back down, and reached behind Luke for my panties. But just as I was retrieving them, he snatched them out of my hand, bringing them to his nose for a deep inhale.

"These are mine, now," he said after huffing them, and stuffed them into his pocket.

Well then.

The stall door rattled again. "Dude. I have your car keys, and Brant and I *will* leave without your asses," Teague warned.

Luke's hand flew to his front pocket. "Shit. Left my keys on the bar."

He looked me up and down to make sure I was presentable and yanked the door open.

I was a little disappointed at being interrupted, but a party was a party.

"You bastard," Teague said, play-punching him in the arm.

Then he turned to me. "Our little Aspen. Having some fun on your beach weekend are ya?" he asked, slinging an arm around my shoulder.

"Sure am, Teague. Having a great time. And where might we be going now?"

We returned to the bar where we found Brant. The pitcher of beer had been drained, and I noticed someone had polished off my beer, as well.

Damn.

Teague threw some money on the bar, and clapped his hands together, his wild mane of hair bouncing around his face. "We just got invited to a party at probably the biggest, fanciest house in Southampton."

"Fancier even than Lake's?" I asked, as we headed for the car.

Teague waved his hand. "Hell yeah. Hers will look like a salt box in comparison."

This time, Brant took my hand, and led me to the backseat to sit with him. But as I got in, I had a question.

"Guys. Can I go like this? I mean, I kind of look like a schlub, you know?"

Brant looked me up and down, his gaze resting on

where the hem of my dress had slightly ridden up when I'd fastened my seat belt. "You look fine as you are. But if you want to change, that's fine, too."

Teague looked over from the front seat as Luke pulled out of the lot. "I bet your boss has some nice duds at her house."

Of course. But did I dare wear anything of hers?

Would she even know?

"You're right! Let's go."

I took risks! I could seize the day!

I was *so* not boring.

When we arrived back at Lake's, I ran straight to her closet. I didn't expect much to be there since she didn't spend a lot of time there, but I figured she might have a few things.

And *did* she.

"Oh. My. God," I breathed, pulling a creamy silk charmeuse dress out of her closet and holding it up to myself.

The dress had spaghetti straps and was narrow through the bodice, flaring out at the bottom. It might be a bit much for the beach, but when else would I get to wear something like this?

Still holding the dress, I turned to face the mirror in the corner, and found the three guys standing in the bedroom doorway.

Someone whistled long and low. I wasn't sure who. Didn't care either.

When I saw their expressions, I nearly melted with the admiring approvals their handsome faces wore. If this dress worked for them, it worked for me, too. And I didn't even have it on yet.

I started to change but the guys were still standing there. Granted, they'd already seen me in my panties, but I wasn't even wearing those any longer, thanks to Luke's affinity for undies.

I waved them away like annoying gnats. "You can leave me now. I have to get ready."

They groaned but left, pulling the door closed behind themselves.

I slipped into Lake's dress and I had to say, I didn't think I'd ever felt more beautiful in my life. But I realized all I had to wear were my clunky platforms.

Did Lake wear the same shoe size I did?

I ran back to her closet.

Holy shit, now I was going to wear her shoes.

But I was out of luck. Her shoes were way too small for me to wear. So, I decided, fuck it. I pulled a pair of flip flops out of my duffel, and paired them with the silk dress.

But not before I saw a tattered little notebook tucked onto an upper shelf of the closet.

Shit. Was that what I thought it was?

I had to jump to reach it, but when I pulled it down, several loose pages fluttered out.

Those loose pages?

My drawings. The ones I'd done for Lake. Which she said weren't usable.

I'd suspected she'd been stealing my designs. Did this prove it?

I couldn't be one-hundred percent. But I was pretty close.

Fucking bitch.

In a flash of red-hot anger, I swept my arm through everything hanging in her closet, pulling it all onto the floor. Then, for good measure, I stomped on it with my flip flops.

"What the hell is going on in there?" Teague yelled, sticking his head into the room. "C'mon. Time to go."

Right. I had a party to get to. In Lake's dress. And afterward, I'd come back and sleep in Lake's bed. And when I was ready, I'd drive Lake's car back to Manhattan.

If she had an issue with any of that? She could suck my dick.

"Coming, guys!" I sang and ran for the door.

Holy shit.

Would you look at that?

You are one gorgeous woman.

I rolled my eyes. "You guys are crazy. Let's go."

5

The party was just as glittery as Teague promised, with beautiful people everywhere. They were well-dressed, attractive, smiling, and seemed to have no end of fascinating things to talk about.

And I felt damn good in my dress and flip flops, accompanied by the three best-looking guys there.

As soon as we arrived, Teague was shaking hands and slapping backs.

Luke turned to me. "I'm off to find something to drink. You guys want anything?"

"Aspen, a drink?" Brant asked.

"Sure," I said slowly, looking around the room. "I'll have a glass of… that pink champagne everyone has," I said, pointing.

He nodded and turned to Brant.

"The usual for me, man. Just a beer."

I turned to Brant, happy to have a solo moment with the clean-cut one of the trio. "So, you've lived here all your life?"

He laughed and looked down at his shoes for a moment, like he was embarrassed. "I can hardly believe it myself. But it's not a bad place. Beautiful, no matter what the season, even in the middle of winter with wicked storms blowing in. I don't think I could ever live far from the ocean," he said, looking out our host's giant living room window to the beach, where all you could see in the dark was the white foam of the waves breaking on the beach.

It was hard to look away, the rhythm of the moving water so mesmerizing. "If you can believe it, I'd never even seen the ocean before I moved to New York. As soon as I got here, I took the train to the Jersey shore to see if the Atlantic was everything I'd heard."

He looked down at me, his dark eyes holding mine, and flicked a stray piece of hair out of my face. "And?"

I thought back to that day, and how I'd decided I could never go back to the Midwest for any reason other than to visit.

"I was… speechless. Honestly. I couldn't believe it. Water for as far as you can see. You hear people talk about the ocean. But in person it's completely different."

He smiled and a dimple I'd not noticed before popped into view. Like he needed to be better-looking.

"Hey, want to see something else really amazing?" he asked.

I shrugged. "More amazing than this? You've got me curious."

He held out his hand and after a moment's hesitation, I took it. Why not?

I followed him as he wove through the crowd, stopping every now and then to say hello to someone, until we reached a door off the kitchen that looked like it led to a basement.

"Is this where you take me to the bowels of the house and lock me up for all eternity?" I laughed.

He squeezed my hand. "Something like that."

He opened the door and reached to turn a light on. When I joined him on the other side, I saw we were not descending into some nasty old basement. No, it was more of a spa, if I could name it anything, and at the bottom of the stairs was a beautiful, indoor, blue-green swimming pool illuminated by a couple dim, overhead lights.

"Oh my god. Look at this," I said, making a three-hundred-sixty-degree turn to take it all in.

"My old man worked on this house," Brant said, taking me through the indoor pool room.

"Really? Your dad works on houses?" I asked.

"Yeah. Well, he doesn't just work on houses. He *builds* them."

I looked up at him. "So are you saying you live in a house like this?"

He laughed modestly. "No. Our house is more like… your boss's house."

Holy shit.

"Then why do you guys swim over there? You have your own pools," I said.

He led me to a ledge of rocks that created a small waterfall and sat me down. "We like to… change things up every now and then."

Brant crouched before me, sliding my dress above

my ankles, and pulled off one of my flip flops. Running his fingers up the side of my calf, his touch was so light it tickled, and I had to squirm to remain still.

How could I have the same chemistry with this man, as I did with Luke and Teague? My head was spinning. It didn't seem right, and yet I couldn't name a single thing wrong with it.

Brant slipped off my other flip flop, and slipping his hands under my dress, pushed the soft fabric to my knees. Once they were bare, he put his hands on each and slowly parted them, finally breaking eye contact to find that I wasn't wearing panties.

"Look at that," he murmured in a low, growly voice. "What a pretty pussy we have here."

The night air whispered across flesh that was usually covered up and hidden away. It was amazing, and even more so when Brant ran a finger through my wet folds, stopping to dip inside me, and then run the moisture back up to my clit, which he circled with his thumb.

I leaned back onto hard rocks, barely registering any discomfort, just reveling in being with a gorgeous man in an amazing house, wearing one of my boss's expensive silk dresses.

If I paused long enough to think about it all, I'd run out of there, scared shitless.

So, I didn't.

Next I knew, Brant had pushed my legs all the way open and buried his face between my legs, running his tongue up and down my aching pussy, pausing to zero in on my clit, and then licking me top to bottom again.

Without thinking about it, I reached for his head and ran my nails over his scalp, pulling him closer.

"Oh fuck, that feels nice," I moaned.

When he slipped one, and then two fingers inside me, I bucked my hips forward for more. I wanted it deeper, and I wanted it harder.

And I wanted it now.

"Oh god, I'm coming," I cried, clamping my hand over my mouth to keep my screams from reaching the party.

"Oh yeah, baby, come on my hand," Brant said, watching me.

I gripped his shoulder with my one free hand and squeezed, digging my nails in so hard I knew there'd be marks later. But I needed some way to bleed off the energy exploding out of my every pore.

"Oh god stop, Brant, stop. I need a break," I gasped, overcome by sensation.

He got to his feet and began to open his shorts. But I stopped him, and took over.

"Let me," I said, swatting his hands away.

When Brant's shorts were unzipped, they fell to the floor with a thud. He whipped his T-shirt off over his head and there he stood, gloriously and heart-breakingly naked and beautiful. If I hadn't been so ready to suck his cock, I might have looked at him for a moment longer, my eyes filling with tears.

But I was not feeling patient.

I fisted his cock lightly, running my palm from root to tip, over his head, and back down again. Tilting my head up, I found him looking down at me with a small smile. I smiled back, and he ran his fingers along my jaw before taking the back of my head and pulling my head down on him.

He was long and thick, but I took as much of him as I could before he bumped the back of my throat. I continued to hold him at his base, and moved my tongue and lips over him, slowly picking up speed.

"Play with yourself, baby. Play with that pussy using your free hand," he demanded.

I slipped my fingers between the folds Brant had just had his face between, still puffy and dripping with my excitement. I worked myself at the same pace I worked him, wondering if I could bring us both off at the same time.

It turned out I almost could.

Brant began to thrust his hips into my face. He swelled inside my mouth one last time, spurting his load until I couldn't take any more and let it run down my chin. When he slowed, a thunderbolt struck me and I stiffened, pushing him out of my mouth so I could scream through my own explosion.

He took me by the hand and we collapsed on a lounge chair together, trying to catch our breath, when from the direction of the stairs came a slow applause.

What? Who the hell was clapping?

I weakly lifted my head to see Teague standing there, smiling broadly.

Of course it was Teague.

"Fucking hot, you two. That was quite a show," he said.

Brant chuckled. "Sucks to be you, dude."

Teague sauntered over in our direction, studying my now-rumpled dress and smeared make up. "Oh, I don't know. Does our little Aspen have any gas left in her tank?" he asked, putting his fingers on either side of my chin and turning my head in his direction.

"Depends on where you wanna go, Teague," I said, lifting my chin.

He brought me to my feet and turned me to face Brant. "Bend forward, honey. Brace your hands on Brant's knees."

Still buzzing from my orgasm of only a few minutes before, I was happy to oblige, and when I did, Teague eased my feet back so I was bent at a ninety-degree angle, ass up in the air. He lifted my dress to my waist, and ran his fingers through my slick folds.

"Got her nice and ready for me, didn't you, Brant?" he rasped.

Oh, what his dirty talk did to me.

"Hey, man. I aim to please."

Teague's fingers slowly parted my pussy lips and between them, the head of his cock slipped back and forth. "You okay, baby? You ready for me?" he asked.

I might have just come from my own hand, but I wanted to come again. And hard.

"Please, Teague. Please fuck me," I begged.

In one slick movement, he was buried inside me, gripping my ass so hard I knew there'd be marks later, but with enough purchase to drive in and out of me with a fury that was almost scary.

Brant, in front of me, put his hands on either side of my face, his gaze glued to mine as I started coming again. "You're so beautiful, baby. Let me see you come, c'mon, come again all over Teague's cock," he whispered so only I could hear it.

This time, my orgasm was different, starting at my core and firing to the lengths of my limbs like an out-of-control shockwave. I shook, barely able to hold myself up without the support of both guys, and when an orgasm broke, it was like being hit by a truck, battering and bruising me until I was nothing like I had been before our tryst.

Seriously. By the time Teague exploded inside me, I couldn't see, hear, or speak. I could only feel.

And I felt fucking great.

6

BUT I WASN'T TOO OUT OF IT TO HEAR FOOTSTEPS
pounding down the stairs toward the indoor pool,
where Teague and Brant had just finished with me.

Or should I say, I'd finished with them?

"Guys, guys," Luke hollered. He stopped short when
he saw us in various stages of undress, shook his head,
and laughed. "Jesus. Guys, get your shit together. A fight
broke out and the cops are on their way."

I lifted my head. "So? We haven't done anything
wrong? Why should we leave?"

Teague jumped up and tucked himself back into his
shorts then ran his fingers through his hair. "You don't
understand. When a party has this many people, and if
they want to question everyone, you could get stuck
here till sunrise."

Okay then.

Luke pulled me to my feet while Brant tossed
me my flip flops. I straightened my dress out as
best I could, and we headed for the door that led

out to the beach rather than going back through the house.

But Teague stopped. "Hold on. I just thought of something."

Brant sighed in exasperation. "Teague, man, c'mon. Let's go."

But Teague was already halfway up the stairs. When he reached the top, he bellowed at full volume. "Hey, everyone, party will continue at the house down the road with the gray shingles. Meet us there!"

Then he bolted back down the stairs toward us and ran out the back door.

Oh my god.

Please tell me I'd just misheard him.

Did he just invite the entire party back to Lake's house? My boss's house? That I was supposed to be departing from on the 8am bus, which would later in the day have a private showing by a real estate agent?

No. How silly. Surely he was referring to a different house. With gray shaker shingles. Just down the road.

I ran out the door after him and caught him by the shoulder, whipping him around with all my strength. When he turned and realized I was the one who'd done it, he was as surprised as I was by my fury.

"Are you fucking kidding?" I screamed.

It didn't matter that he'd just fucked my brains out and given me so many orgasms I'd lost count.

He was messing with my livelihood. And I couldn't have that. Especially since I was capable of fucking up quite nicely on my own.

But he wasn't discouraged. Of course not. Because

he was Teague, the good-looking guy who charmed his way into any situation. Including my panties.

He grabbed my hand. "Aspen, it will be fine. These are nice, respectable people. And Brant and Luke will clean up in the morning."

That earned him a smack in the back of the head at Luke's hand.

I looked at him and Brant. Surely they had more common sense than their friend. But they didn't back me up. Not exactly.

"Aspen is now realizing what a dick Teague is," Brant said. "But look. People are pouring out of the party and into their cars. I think we'd better get to the house before they do."

I looked at the headlights of Porsches, Audis, and one or two Hummers, all coming to life and peeling away from the lawns they'd parked all over.

To head to Lake's.

"All right. Let's go," I said, breaking into a run.

Thank god I'd worn my flip flops.

We arrived at Lake's to find several guys at the front door holding cases of beer and bottles of booze. I hesitantly opened the door, because they looked like they wouldn't hesitate to find a way inside the house anyway, and stepped aside as people streamed in. In the shuffle, I got separated from the guys, so I pulled a chair to block the entrance to the upstairs of the house, and opened the back door in the hope that people would just swarm the deck and the pool.

"This way, people," I hollered, pointing to the back of the house.

And it worked.

Thank god.

"It'll be fine, Aspen," Luke said in my ear.

"Oh. Where did you come from?"

He pointed across the room. "I was over there, watching you take charge," he said, running a finger down the front of my rumpled dress, stopping to tease my erect nipple.

I casually placed a hand on the credenza next to me so he wouldn't see me wobble. But it didn't work. He knew he had me.

The bastard.

"I was kind of pissed that we were interrupted in the restroom, and then I found you with Brant and Teague," he said quietly, continuing to rub my nipple through my silky dress with his rough thumb.

I was trying to pay attention to the party around me since it was being held in a house I was essentially responsible for, at least for a few more hours.

Shit, I'd leave right now if the car were ready. Say I had no idea what happened.

They must have broken in. I don't know a thing. Sorry!

But I couldn't do that, not only because I had to wait for Lake's BMW to be fixed, but also because Luke's touch was drawing me in, like a fly to a spider web. There was no escape.

Not that I wanted one.

Fuck it. Everyone else was having fun. Why not me.

I looked down at Luke's agonizing touch, then back up at him, coyly batting my eyelashes. "Sorry 'bout that, Luke. I didn't forget about you. I just got kind of…

distracted," I cooed, running my flat palm up his T-shirt and over his rocky chest.

He clearly did a lot more than clean pools to maintain a body like his.

I looked behind him, to the backyard, where people, both clothed and unclothed, were splashing around in Lake's pool.

"I have an idea," I whispered in his ear.

I took his hand and let him out the back door and to the little pool house I'd spotted earlier in the day. It looked like a cross between a fancy shed and a guest cottage. We wove between the partiers, many of whom were in various stages of undress, and slipped into the small building.

I led him over to a colorful sofa, where I lifted what was left of Lake's silk dress over my head, and tossed it aside. There I sat, completely nude, with Luke just before me. I parted my thighs slightly so he could stand between them, and ran my hands up over my breasts, my gaze locked to his.

He growled lightly as his hands moved to his fly.

"Your T-shirt," I said, gesturing with my chin. I kept playing with my tits as he slowly grabbed opposite corners of his shirt, lifting it over his head, and dropping it onto the pile with my dress.

I'd seen him shirtless earlier in the day, but now that I was close up, I could really appreciate his bulky pecs, and the hollow running down the center of his abdomen in between the mountains of his six-pack muscles. I took my hands from my own chest, and ran them over his, warm and smooth and strong.

He tackled his fly and in moments his shorts and boxers were puddled around his feet. His hard cock hung heavy and low, bouncing lightly as if trying to grab my attention.

And grab my attention, it did.

I ran my fingers up his velvety shaft until I reached his cockhead, bulbous in my fist. A drop of precum wet my hand, which I brought up to my mouth to taste.

Luke groaned with approval, and with a hand on either side of my head, wove his fingers into my hair. Holding fistfuls in each, he pulled me until his erection bounced against my lips.

I took hold of him at the root of his dick and ran my tongue around his head and then its ridge, enjoying the way he jolted when I closed my mouth over him.

"God, baby, yes, suck me like that. Good girl. Oh that's so fucking good," he said in a hoarse whisper. He let go of my hair when I took him as deeply as I could, his hands wandering to my breasts, now sensitive and begging for attention.

Even though he was almost to the back of my throat, I was still holding a good bit of him in my hand. My other hand took hold of his balls. He started to shake, pumping his hips into my face as I took him deeper, when I heard a sound at the door.

But I didn't care. He was about to come, and I wanted to swallow every last bit of what he had to give me. And a moment later, after swelling one more time, his hot, salty cum flooded my mouth, running down my chin and onto my breasts when I couldn't take any more.

Someone plopped onto the sofa right next to me and while I was still licking Luke clean, I glanced over to see him stroking his erection through the open fly of his shorts.

"Oh my. Look at Brant's hard cock," I teased when Luke stepped away.

"And look at you, my little beach baby," he growled, reaching between my legs with one hand and pulling me in for a kiss with his other.

His lips were hot and sensuous, and as soon as his fingers dipped into my wet pussy, he pulled them out and pressed one against my lips. "Taste yourself, baby. There you go," he said as I eagerly sucked.

He took his finger back and pushed his shorts out of the way. "Since you're so wet, baby, come on over here. I'm thinking you'd like to sit on my dick."

As I stood, Teague joined us and closed the pool house door. Now I had all three guys.

I straddled Brant's lap with one knee on either side of his hips, and rubbed my pussy along his long, thick cock.

"Fuckin' A," he mumbled, his eyes closing, his head falling back onto the sofa.

"Yeah, you're right. I want your dick."

I placed a hand on each of his shoulders and began to lower myself. I stopped for a moment to tease his cockhead, and shouted from the delicious sensation when he seized my hips and pulled me all the way down, impaling me.

My head dropped into the crook of his neck at suddenly being so full of the long, thick cock of a gorgeous strong man. And to top it off, two of his equally handsome friends were only inches away, watching with admiration as I slowly slid up and down.

I'd never had a threesome, never mind a foursome, but so far I could report it was pretty fucking hot. It was like a roller coaster ride at a theme park. You knew you were in for something thrilling, but you never knew what lay around each corner. Thrills and surprises abounded, and you laughed and screamed through all of them.

And when I say these guys were full of surprises, I was not exaggerating. As I straddled Brant, my entire body humming as my pussy engulfed and then released him, a warm breath fell on the back of my neck. It was followed by a brush of soft lips, which traveled down my shoulders to my spine. Brant's hands were already gripping my waist, but when a new set of hands cupped my ass cheeks and parted them, I didn't have the where-withal to wonder what was next.

I was going with it.

These men could do whatever they wanted with me. They made me feel like a million bucks, and I wanted nothing more than to do the same for them. I was driven by a need to please and be pleased, and no amount of rational thinking was going to get in my way, even if it was charging through my brain a thousand miles per hour.

Fuck everybody and everything else in the world. I was living in that very moment, and felt like I'd been born again. I could do anything. I was sexy, smart, and capable of handling my shit.

Teague—I knew it was Teague because I'd reached back and fingered his mop of hair—ran his tongue over my asshole, inches from where Brant's hard dick impaled me. I didn't know guys did stuff that got them so, um… *close* to each other, but it didn't seem to slow anyone down.

And for that, I was grateful as fuck, because it was the best feeling ever. Seriously. I'd had a couple guys hint around at backdoor play, but I had no trust that they'd bother to make it feel good.

Teague—like his friends—was clearly taking things to a completely new level.

7

With a hand on my lower back, Teague slowed my bouncing on Brant's dick. He then pressed something small but hard against my asshole, and when it popped into my bum, I recognized it as his thumb. He gradually entered me with it, and while it felt strange for a moment, it quickly turned into a crazy, intense sensation that heightened the feeling of the big dick in my pussy.

What would it feel like to have more than just a thumb back there? Would it hurt? Or feel so good I'd lose my mind?

I was willing to find out.

"Yeah, dude, that's it," Luke growled from behind me. "Stretch that little asshole."

His filthy, dirty talk and raspy voice unleashed a guttural cry from my throat. I looked over my shoulder at Teague and Luke watching me get fucked while my asshole was prepared, and I swear I'd never seen anything more desirable.

"Give me more, Teague," I breathed, raising my ass as best I could while keeping Brant inside me.

"You heard the lady," Brant said between groans. "Guess my dick is just not enough."

I play-slapped him while giving him a passionate kiss to show him he was wrong. "It's perfect. But I'm feeling greedy," I laughed.

Behind me, Teague spat, and next I knew, something much bigger than his thumb was pressed against my asshole. Brant slowed our movements and Luke grabbed a fistful of my hair, turning me to kiss him. His tongue aggressively invaded my mouth just as Teague pushed harder, until the head of his dick was in my behind.

Holy fuck. There was no describing the sensation of having something in both my pussy and ass, while being passionately kissed. I moaned into Luke's mouth and he pulled back, smiling.

"You like it, baby?" he asked.

My eyes fell closed. All I could do was nod.

Teague continued holding my cheeks open and with his thumbs, massaged the area around my asshole as if trying to get me to relax. I guess it worked, because he inched farther inside me until I exploded in a violent orgasm that took all three guys to restrain me.

My head bucked and my shoulders shook while I pushed back and forth on both Brant and Teague, taking each of them as deeply as I could. I pounded the sofa back with my fists and screamed until I was hoarse. One orgasm after another lit me on fire, and the only thing that snapped me out of it was the screaming and shouting that suddenly arose in Lake's backyard.

"What the hell is that?" one of the guys mumbled as we quickly disentangled ourselves.

Which I was not happy about.

We watched Luke run to the door of the pool house. When he pulled it open, his eyes widened.

"Hate to tell you guys, but the cops are here," he said, starting to close the door.

But before he could, one police officer stuck a huge flashlight against the doorjamb, blocking it from closing. Teague, Brant, and I scrambled to pull ourselves back together, but I felt like I was swimming through mud. The guys saw me struggling, and Teague threw me a beach towel draped over a folded lawn chair. I wrapped myself just as a cop stuck his head inside.

"Okay, guys, party's over," he said, ignoring the fact that what we'd just been doing was painfully obvious. "Get yourselves dressed and get out here."

I scooped what was left of Lake's silk dress off the pool house floor and pulled it over my head. I had to wear something, and a beach towel wasn't going to cut it. And as I did, I pushed aside a small curtain and saw the yard swarming with people running in all directions like they'd committed a serious crime and were about to go to prison for life.

I had to keep from laughing out loud. I guess that's what an overload of orgasms will do to you.

One skinny dipping guy had even picked up his clothes without bothering to dress before running off, his butt cheeks jiggling as he frantically ran in one direction and then another.

We left the pool house and followed the cop who was waiting for us on the patio.

"You all are trespassing. You're going to have to leave," he said in a bored voice.

I guess I'd be bored too, policing in a town where the worst crime was crashing pool parties. He was probably pissed he hadn't been invited.

"Oh, I'm supposed to be here. This is my boss's house," I said, looking at the wet footprints that had been tracked from the pool and onto the floors.

That should mop up easily. Right?

"Do you have any proof of that?"

"C'mon Dave," Brant said, "we can vouch for her. She works for Lake LaRenne."

My head whipped in his direction. "You *know* this policeman?"

He nodded. "Of course. We graduated high school together."

Teague dropped a casual arm around my shoulder. "It's a small town, Aspen. Those of us who've spent any length of time here know pretty much everyone."

"Yeah," the cop said, putting his hands on his hips and looking over the guys. "I know all these guys. I wouldn't be at all surprised if they were the ones to talk you into having a big party in a place where you probably weren't supposed to."

"Oh, um, well, yeah…" I managed to say.

I didn't want to get anyone in trouble.

He took a step closer and looked down on me. "Am I

right? That you did not have your boss's permission to throw a party here? Miss, I am supposed to notify the homeowner when something like this happens."

My stomach sank. Why did I keep fucking up? On top of everything, I was wearing what I was sure was an ungodly expensive dress that was now covered in stains and holes, and Lake's floor was covered in muddy, grassy footprints.

I opened my mouth again, but thankfully, before I said something to get myself in even more trouble, Luke spoke up.

"Dave, can you help us out just this once?" he said. "Forget this ever happened?"

"Oh yes, that would be great," I babbled, "you see, my boss is selling and an agent is holding some private showings tomorrow—"

Dave scoffed. "This place is a mess. But I'll leave you guys to it. Just no more noise for tonight. We're getting tired of these calls, and the season is just barely underway."

Brant extended his hand. "Thanks, Dave. See you at softball Wednesday night."

As soon as the cop was gone, I turned to Brant. "You play *softball* with this guy? Are you serious?"

"Sure do," he said.

I plopped onto a lounge chair. "Oh my god, I am tired."

Luke grabbed the spot at the end of my chair. "Guess we wore you out, huh?"

I couldn't help but smile. "You know it," I said, squirming a little in my seat. But I couldn't think about that stuff now. I had to be responsible again. "Guys, I am totally stressing about cleaning this place up. I'm supposed to be out of here at 8 am."

Brant started picking up empty beer cans. "Aspen, you know that's not gonna happen. For one, you gotta wait for Lake's car."

I started to bury my face in my hands, overwhelmed.

But Luke pulled me to my feet. "Look. Let's all get some sleep. We'll get up early, and start cleaning. It's really not so bad."

Ugh. I hoped to have his casual clarity after a few hours' sleep.

"Sounds like you guys have done this before," I said.

They looked at each other with sly smiles.

Because, of course. Gorgeous, socially-blessed guys like this got away with everything.

Someone like me, from bumfuck Iowa, of average looks, and a crappy going-nowhere job in overpriced Manhattan?

Not so much.

Hell, if I jaywalked, I'd probably get a freaking ticket. Maybe even imprisoned for life.

I headed for the house and once inside, breathed a sigh of relief that it wouldn't take much more than a wet mop and a little scrubbing to clean the floor.

Thank god the party crashers had headed straight for the backyard. Not that it was without damage. But, as I dragged myself up the stairs, I decided the guys would have to take on that piece. I had no idea how to clean vomit off a pool deck, extract a lacy pair of thong panties from the pool filter, or even out the broken branches on the bush where two people had been making out.

To my thinking, if they could get a cop off my ass, they could do just about anything. And that's what I was counting on.

I turned to see the guys hanging out downstairs and it occurred to me to wonder where they were going to sleep. After what we'd all just done, it seemed like spending the night together was what would follow, like it did after most hook-ups. But since I'd arrived in Southampton, what else about my life had been predictable or normal?

"What are you doing?" I asked, pausing halfway up the stairs.

I won't lie. I was kind of hoping one or all of them wanted to snuggle with me overnight. It would be so nice to have some warm, strong arms around me. On the other hand, I couldn't expect all three guys to cram into one bed with me. That would just be greedy.

Or not.

Uncharacteristically, Teague shuffled his feet and looked around the room. I'd never seen him express even a tiny bit of uncertainty.

Interesting.

"Well, um," he started, "I guess we were waiting for an invitation."

What?

As if sharing a bed overnight were more intimate than how they'd all fucked me minutes earlier.

But his words warmed me.

I stood there on the stairs with the three of them

looking back at me, waiting, and I realized I was somehow different than when I'd arrived that morning.

How change could take place that fast was beyond me, but I wasn't looking a gift horse in the mouth. It was as if the moment I'd decided to say to hell with it and take Lake's car to the Hamptons, without even knowing it, I'd altered the trajectory of my life. I'd had no idea at the time, but thinking back just a few hours, that was a balls-out move for me. I'd needed to shake shit up.

And I did.

I was in the middle of something I couldn't identify, but it was exciting. Scary as fuck, but exciting.

I just had to get through it with my head on straight.

While these thoughts flashed through my mind in an instant, I knew I was on the brink of something big. Something that was going to allow me to grab life by the balls without shame or embarrassment.

Like Teague, Luke, and Brant did.

I pulled my shoulders back and puffed out my chest, just like the guys did when they showed the world they could do fucking anything. "One of you may join me, or all of you may. I will let you decide."

I headed up the stairs, leaving three guys behind me, grinning wildly.

8

_____

I DIDN'T KNOW WHETHER THEY FLIPPED A COIN, DREW
straws, or played Rock Paper Scissors, but before I was
even under the covers in Lake's luxurious bedroom,
Teague had bounded up the stairs, stripped, jumped in
bed, and propped his head up on a pillow, smiling.

And it felt damn good.

I pulled the fluffy down comforter up to my chin.

"I'm not really tired," Teague said, flipping onto his
side to face me.

"No?"

I guess I was kind of wound up, myself.

Seriously, how does one just drop off to sleep after a
day like I'd had?

"Where did Brant and Luke go?" I asked.

"I think they crashed on lounge chairs out back.
They like that sort of thing," he said.

It was funny to see these guys, how carefree and
playful they were, even though they were the same age
as me. Had our lives collided for a reason?

"What's your boss like?" Teague asked, running a soft finger down my arm.

I sighed. She wasn't hard to describe. Not at all. Which actually made it tricky to talk about her without sounding like a massive cliché. But she *was* a cliché. "Typical power bitch," I said. "Sucks up to those with money and power, like her investors, and shits on people below her, like me. She's so lacking insight she has no idea how insulting she is, nor how badly she makes herself look. She's like a beautiful piece of fruit that, when you bite into it, is rotten on the inside."

He let out a low whistle and was silent for a moment. "Sounds like a real winner."

"I know. The worst of it is, she steals my designs after telling me they're no good."

I started dozing off, sad that my last waking thought of the night was about the very person I wanted to forget.

Teague scoffed. "Fuck that bitch. I'm glad we're chilling in her house. I've got an idea."

I gasped, startling back to wakefulness. "Huh?"

"Can you prove she stole your stuff?" Teague asked.

I'd asked myself this a million times. Even though I'd found her notebook in the closet, I wasn't so sure. And if I could, what would I do with the information? Who'd believe me over her?

And where was Teague going with this? He had a wealthy father and a nice home to live in on both coasts. He could afford to burn bridges. Put people in their places.

Me? Not so much.

68

I was beholden to someone who could take advantage of me pretty much any way she wanted, short of breaking the law.

But not breaking my spirit.

"Yeah, I probably could, but who would I prove it *to*? Who's gonna take my word over hers? She's well-connected. Everyone loves her. I'm just one of her peons."

"Did you say… you were here to pick up a laptop she'd left behind?" he asked, his finger now running down my bare breast.

I gasped, Teague's touch sending me back to a place —one I wished I could never leave.

"Y… yeah, her laptop is downstairs. But I'm sure it's password protected. It's not like we could get into it or something."

Teague scoffed. "We'll see about that," he said, suddenly moving.

He threw the covers off us both and pushed my legs up to my shoulders. In the small bit of moonlight coming into the room, I watched his eyes travel hungrily over my body, stopping at my most private parts. Which, of course, he'd already licked, sucked, and fucked.

He ran two fingers between my pussy lips and my head sank back into the pillow.

Oh god.

While he rendered me helpless, he continued with his train of thought, which I could barely follow. "I know a lot of people, Aspen. All us guys do. We'll check it out tomorrow."

Thank god, because he'd positioned his cock right at the opening to my pussy, and even though I'd just been thoroughly fucked, all I could think about was how I wanted it again.

And as if he could read my mind, he plunged deep inside me, until his pelvis pressed against my clit and his balls banged my ass.

But this time it was different. Different from the first party we'd attended, and different from the pool house.

This time, he placed his hands on either side of my face, and as he moved his hips, his thick cock stroking my insides, he looked directly into my eyes.

"Beautiful. You are beautiful," he breathed.

His gaze was so painfully intimate that for a moment I had to close my eyes. I was afraid of losing myself, of getting absorbed into some weird vortex of passion I couldn't return from. But as his fingers wove into my hair, he pressed his lips to mine and I opened my eyes again. I didn't want to miss a thing.

We moved together as we kissed and with a few more strokes, my umpteenth orgasm for the day lit me like a firecracker. I arched into him, gasping, pulling on his ass for more. I was insatiable, and so, apparently, was he.

When he was finally ready to explode, he pulled out and came all over my chest and stomach. I opened my eyes to see if he was still looking at me.

He was.

It was like he knew what I wanted. He'd taken my mind off the negative thoughts nagging at it and now I could sleep in peace. I'd worry about all the shit on my mind tomorrow, when I woke up.

And that tomorrow came way too fast, when I heard a car crunch into the circular driveway in front of Lake's house.

I bolted up in bed to look out the window, then pulled on my one dress that hadn't been destroyed. I opened the back window and hissed until Luke and Brant stirred on their lounge chairs.

"Guys," I called quietly. "The agent's here. Go hide."

They sat up, squinting at me in the morning sun, and in seconds, they dashed into the pool house.

I turned to Teague. "Wait here and don't make a sound. I'll get rid of her."

I raced down the stairs and pulled the door open just as the agent was pushing her key into the lock.

Her eyes widened, and she jumped back. "Oh my," she gasped.

I smoothed a hand over my hair when I saw her looking me up and down. "Hi, I'm so sorry for startling you. I'm Aspen, Lake's assistant."

She shifted, trying to look past me into the house.

"Yeah, the place is a bit of a mess," I said, glancing over my shoulder but still not letting her enter.

"Um, I was told you were leaving early this morning, and that the house would be empty and ready to go," she said as a half-question, half-statement.

I nodded cheerfully. "You're right. You're absolutely right. I would be gone by now except the house needed cleaning. You see, it seems like some people, probably kids, broke in and had a party. I've been cleaning up since I arrived. I have a bit more to do so figured I'd stay as long as I needed to. I should have called you. I'm so sorry I didn't," I said, rolling my eyes at my own stupidity.

I laughed to lighten the moment, but also planted my hands on my hips to show I was serious about getting the situation under control.

She tried to look past me again, so I gave her a couple more inches of view into the living room while still blocking her.

"There's no serious damage, thank goodness. Just trash and some basic cleaning that a little elbow grease will take care of."

She frowned. "Well, I was supposed to show the house today. When do you think it will be ready? Lake is really eager to sell."

I nodded like I was completely in the loop. "I know. She really is. I feel so badly that someone did this to her. Just awful. But I'll tell you, I am confident I can finish the job today. Could you maybe come back tomorrow with your clients? Would they be okay with that?"

She pressed her lips together, thinking. Then, she glanced at her watch, and pulled out her phone. "Let me make a couple calls, okay?" she asked, stepping back from the door.

Under normal circumstances, it would have been polite to invite her in while she made her calls but I didn't want her too close to the scene of the crime.

"I'll give you some privacy here," I said cheerfully, and I closed the front door.

I glanced through the glass in the door and saw her

break into a smile as she undoubtedly got her rich and important client on the phone. As she schmoozed, I ran to the kitchen. Rustling under the sink, I pulled out yellow kitchen gloves, a large sponge, and a bottle of Spic 'n Span. Just as she finished her calls, I returned to the front door, my cleaning supplies in hand.

"All good?" I asked with a bright smile.

She nodded slowly, still looking a bit confused. "Um, yes. I can bring them all by tomorrow. Please make sure the house is in perfect shape though, won't you?"

I nodded fervently. "Oh my god, of course. I want Lake's house to sell fast just like you do!"

I looked at the agent, who had dollar signs in her eyes. I, on the other hand, didn't get a damn thing whether the house sold or not.

"So, we'll see you tomorrow?" I chirped.

She shrugged. "Yes, you will.

I sank against the front door after I closed it, listening carefully for the crunch of the agent's shoes on the gravel, and for her car to pull away. It wasn't until she was gone that I could breathe easily again.

"Guys," I hollered, watching Teague come down the stairs and Brant and Luke return from the pool house.

"I heard the whole thing. The house was broken into! That's classic! Good job, baby." Teague laughed.

"No way," Brant said, joining us in the kitchen. "Is that what you told the agent?" he asked, shaking his head.

I shrugged. "Well, those people here last night *were* party crashers, more or less. And the cop said we were trespassing. So does that count as breaking in?"

Luke took the cleaning supplies from me. "It doesn't matter. What does, is that we have some time to chill and enjoy the pool if we want. She's not coming back until tomorrow and the place will be perfect by then."

Teague ran a finger down my spine, and I shivered even though the kitchen was warm from the morning sun. "And now we can have some fun. If you're up for it?" he asked.

I looked from one guy to the next.

They were all so damn good-looking, and sure as hell had been showing me the time of my life. It could be the last day I'd spend with them, after which I might never see them again.

Even though I'd known them barely twenty-four hours, a pang of sadness washed through me. It was weird to think I'd miss something I'd never really had. I mean, how the hell did that work?

It was stupid. We'd have our last bit of fun, clean up the house, and I'd head back to Manhattan with Lake's car repaired. No one would ever know what had gone down except me and the guys. Lake's house would be sold, she'd forget about Southampton, and Southampton would forget about her.

I'd never forget, though. That was for damn sure.

I pulled my dress over my head, dropping it to the kitchen floor, where I stood naked. "Last one in the pool has to go pick up lunch," I screamed, then ran toward the pool, which I landed in with a giant cannonball.

I didn't care who was last, as long as they joined me.

9

I took a deep breath and swam along the bottom of the pool, breaking through to the surface to gasp for air. As soon as I'd pushed the wet hair off my face, I felt a pair of hands on my bare ass.

"Such a hot little behind you have," Brant growled in my ear.

I laughed and pushed back against him, his hands making way for my cheeks to slide up and down his now-hard cock.

"Jesus. That didn't take long," I said, grinding on him.

"Oh fuck," he moaned. "It doesn't take long when you strip off your dress and run like that."

He reached around and placed his palm on my stomach, then, slowly lowered it to cup my pussy. His middle finger dipped between my lips, wiggling against my slit.

"Damn, baby. You're already nice and slippery."

I think I'd been slippery since the moment I'd met these guys.

I let my head loll back onto his shoulder. "What are we gonna do about that?" I teased.

"I can think of a few things," he said, lifting my feet off bottom of the pool, carrying me toward the edge with his hand still between my legs.

When we reached the stairs in the corner, he positioned me on the second step with my right leg poised on the edge of the pool. Then he pushed me forward, where I held the stairs' railing, and he situated himself behind me. His cocked bounced between my legs as he held me by the waist, and I felt myself opening. I wanted it, and wanted it now.

"How would you like it, baby? Pussy or ass?" he asked in a low, rasping voice.

I'd heard that voice before. It came before a nice, hot, delicious fucking.

Across the yard, I saw Teague and Luke talking in the kitchen. But when they caught a look at what Brant and I were doing, they joined us in the yard, huge grins on their faces.

"I'm fucking watching this. I'll get lunch after," Teague said, plopping into a lounge chair under an oversized umbrella.

Luke did the same, settling in with his hands behind his head, all nice and comfortable for our show.

I'd never been an exhibitionist before, at least not that I was aware of. But having Brant bend me forward until my tits swung, running his finger from my ass to clit and back, in the beautiful sunshine right in front of an audience of two fucking gorgeous men, bathed me in a world of confidence.

"How should he fuck me, guys?" I called across the pool in a naughty, teasing tone.

Yeah, I was naughty. I was a tease.

And these guys loved it.

Teague and Luke looked at each other like kids in a candy store. "Pussy!" Luke hollered.

I glanced over my shoulder. "You heard the man," I said, wiggling against Brant's hard-on.

He took a hand from my waist, and he spat. The motion that followed that told me he was lubing his dick with saliva, something that used to gross me out but now I somehow found incredibly hot, primal, and raw.

Exactly how I felt about getting fucked outdoors with two guys watching.

I lifted my elevated leg higher, begging to have my pussy filled, like a hungry little bird with its mouth wide open.

Brant gripped me again and drove all the way inside me.

I screamed. I couldn't help it.

I couldn't get enough. With him holding me, I could barely move, and had no way to thrust back against him as he drove in and out.

I was at his mercy. Just as he wanted it.

"Oh, that pussy, so good on my cock, so juicy and tight. You're sucking me dry, baby," he growled.

I exploded into an ocean of sensation as he pounded harder and harder, and for a fleeting moment, I wondered what I would do when I was back in Manhattan, far away from these guys.

Surely, they'd just forget about me. And for a moment, my heart hurt.

But I pushed that shit away. I was going to be present, dammit. Worrying about yesterday and tomorrow never did me a bit of goddamn good before, so why should I let that stuff fuck with my head right now? My pussy was being rammed by a gorgeous guy, who also happened to be nice too.

A combo, I had to admit, I was sadly unfamiliar with.

So I was going to enjoy it for every minute I had it.

"Fuck me, Brant, fuck me," I begged, my head bucking as I gripped the railing for purchase.

"Yeah, I'll fuck you," he growled. "Come for me, baby, come for me…"

And as if his words controlled me, a violent orgasm bubbled up from the center of my body, reaching every pore. Wave after wave rolled through me until I lost track of everything around me except the cock making me feel so good. I reached back to my waist and wrapped my fingers around one of Brant's hands, where he was holding me, and he gripped them back without hesitation.

"Oh fuck," he hollered, plunging into me one last time. He held himself there, bending forward to kiss the back of my neck.

We were pulled out of our post-orgasmic reverie by slow applause coming from our audience.

"Nice, dude. Very nice," Teague said.

I looked over, having momentarily forgotten they were even there.

Luke smiled. "That was pretty fucking hot, you two."

Brant helped me out of the pool, sitting me on its edge, and lay down next to me on the warm deck.

"Baby, you about killed me," he said.

"I was about to say the same about you," I replied.

"Hey, guys," Luke called from across the pool.

I managed to turn my head in their direction to see that he and Teague had gotten to their feet.

I waved weakly. Brant didn't even pretend to move.

"We'll be back with lunch," Luke called over his shoulder.

I lay down on the deck next to Brant. The hard concrete was anything but comfortable, but it was warm and about as far as I could move my body at that moment.

Brant slung an arm over me. "What do you think they'll get us?" he asked.

That's right. They hadn't even asked what we wanted. I figured they knew Brant well enough to know what he'd want for his lunch.

Me? Not so much. But on the other hand, I was so hungry they could set just about anything in front of me and I'd devour it.

"I don't know what they're bringing back. But I hope they get a lot of it."

By the time Teague and Luke returned, Brant and I had managed to get our asses over to some lounge chairs. He'd wrapped me in a towel, and then knotted one around his own waist.

"Guys," he called toward his friends, "what took so fucking long?"

Luke threw his hands up in the air. "We went to your

cousin's place but with the weekend traffic, it took forever."

They laid out an assortment of sandwiches, chips, and sodas, and were polite enough to let me choose first.

I started to nibble on turkey and swiss on rye.

"So Aspen," Luke started to say, "I called someone I know. He's a computer whiz."

Teague scoffed. "Call it like it is, dude. The guy's a *hacker.*"

"Whatever, Teague. He doesn't like that term. Anyway, he's coming over later to look at your boss's computer. You know, to see if we can get into it."

Fear coursed through my veins. I wasn't ready. If I did have solid proof that Lake had stolen my designs, how would that feel? And what would I then do with the information? How the hell would I confront someone like her?

"You know guys, about that... I'm not sure I really want to know any more than I already do," I said in a quiet voice.

Luke nodded. "That's fine, Aspen. We don't have to go through with this—"

But Teague cut him off. "Fuck that, Aspen. Your boss is screwing you over. That's bullshit."

I suddenly felt small. Like I was shrinking into nothing. All I could think was to run away like a scared little mouse.

"I... I don't know..."

Brant put a hand on my arm. "Aspen, why don't we see what he finds, and then you can decide. Just because you have proof, it doesn't mean you have to do anything with it."

I looked at the guys, total strangers just twenty-four hours ago. They were the complete package. They really were. All three of them.

I felt a little stab in my heart when I thought of how I'd be leaving them tomorrow. Depending on Lake's car, of course.

I shrugged. "Okay, let's see what he finds."

"You know, Aspen, we had another thought. Something else you might be interested in," Luke said.

Wrinkling my brow, I looked at him. "What? What do you mean?"

Teague shrugged. "Why go back to Manhattan at all? Stay here with us. And come to LA at the end of the summer. My dad knows a lot of people. He can help you get a good job. There are some really good designers in LA. You don't have to be in New York."

I snorted. I really did. And then I snorted again.

"You guys are hilarious. Fucking hilarious."

I looked at each of them, one at a time, to see if they were fucking with me. But their faces were serious.

"This isn't a joke," Luke said. "We discussed it this morning."

I waved him off with another bark of laughter. "Well, that's very nice of you guys. But I have commitments. Responsibilities. A summer of sneaking into other peoples' pools and partying is not really in the cards for me."

Damn. Must be nice.

But everyone had to grow up eventually. Even these guys.

I finished my sandwich and stood. "I'm going to get cleaning. You guys feel free to hang."

With that, I left the three of them by the pool, none of us saying another word.

10

It turned out that, as I'd hoped, the house was pretty easy to clean. I just gathered up all the beer cans and other trash, and mopped the tile floor and wiped down the walls. Then, I moved upstairs to see if any partygoers had made themselves at home up there, even though I'd put a big chair in front of the stairs.

But before I did, I returned to Lake's bedroom and to the closet where I'd found the notebook with my drawings. I sat down on the room's plushy carpet, and paged through it.

Sure, my sketches could have been in her notebook to be used as a reference, but why would she have told me my stuff wasn't good enough yet, then design things so similar? Guess I just didn't want to believe she'd done it.

It looked like she'd swiped the ideas of a number of her staff, too. Not just me. While I supposed that might have made me feel a little better, knowing I wasn't the only victim, it somehow made me madder. It was pretty clear she'd been stealing from people all her career, and made her fortune off other people's talent.

I wanted to kill her. Well, not kill her. But at least beat the shit out of her.

I got to my feet and ran to the stop of the stairs. "Luke," I called.

"Yes, Aspen?" he hollered back.

"Let's get that computer whiz going. I want to see what's on that laptop."

I was pissed and it felt good. I needed to be pissed. It gave me the energy to do what needed to be done.

Something I would have done a long time ago if I'd had the balls.

"No worries, baby. He's already here."

What? I hadn't heard anyone come in.

I ran down the stairs so fast I nearly wiped out, just in time for a guy I'd never seen before to step aside so I could access the laptop he'd gotten into.

"How did you do it?" I breathed.

He just smiled. "We have our ways," he said and excused himself to go.

I went directly to her email and searched for my name. After a bit of snooping, what I found made my stomach turn. Seriously. I thought I might vomit.

It was to our lead designer.

Take Aspen's sketch and superimpose it over one of mine. She'll never know.

Will do, boss. She sure does good work.

No shit. That's why I hired her.

I felt like someone had just hit me on the head and pounded me straight into the ground. My eyes filled with tears, and I grabbed the counter for balance.

"Are you okay, Aspen?" Brant asked, putting an arm around my shoulders.

I tried to shake away the lump in my throat, but it didn't work. "Yeah. I knew it all along. Guess I just needed proof," I said in a breaking voice.

"Sucks, man," Teague said, planting a kiss on my cheek.

Yeah, it sucked. But you know what didn't suck?

These three guys.

What the hell was I moping about?

"I… I don't know how to thank you all. I mean, you've been so nice to me and we met only freaking yesterday. You're just so… so amazing."

Brant pulled me a little closer. "You're pretty amazing, too."

I wasn't sure what they saw in me that was so great. But I didn't mind it. At all.

"Have you thought any more about our offer?" Teague asked, rubbing a warm hand down my back.

The sensation flew right to my core. But I needed to focus, if only for a moment.

"Your offer?" I laughed. "You only mentioned it a couple hours ago. A girl needs more time than that."

He shrugged, and looked at the other guys.

"What? What's up?" I asked.

"Well," Luke started, "turns out my cousin was able to fix the car pretty quickly."

Well shit. Something about that made my pulse race. Like the realization that I had to get out of there and back to the city before Monday morning.

And the thought of that made my stomach churn.

Just then, the phone rang. Lake's landline. Who even had a landline anymore?

I put my finger to my lips as I picked up the phone. "LaRenne residence."

"Aspen!" Lake's voice rang through the line.

She sounded giddy. Guess hot French guy was taking good care of his sugar momma.

"The realtor told me about the house. Thank you for cleaning it all up. I really appreciate that. I can't believe the house was broken into. Crime is just everywhere today, isn't it?" she shrilled.

If she only knew.

"You're welcome, Lake. I am glad to help."

Wait. That sounded like the old Aspen. I didn't want to be her anymore.

"Luckily, Lake, they didn't get your *laptop*," I said.

She giggled at something in the background. "Oh, that would have been terrible. That laptop is very important to me."

I bet.

"Say, Aspen," she continued, "I was considering promoting someone else in the company, but then thought you might be up to the task. You know. What the hell."

For cripe's sake. She was incapable of paying someone a compliment without insulting them at the same time.

"What do you think? Junior designer?" she teased, like she was offering me the moon.

Don't think so, bitch.

Twenty-four hours earlier, I would have done back-flips at an offer like that. I would have cried. I would have been intensely grateful for any little crumb Lake might throw my way. But a lot could change in one day.

"If I'm junior designer, Lake, will you continue to steal my designs?"

There was silence for a moment, and I wondered if we'd been disconnected. I didn't care if we had. I'd said all I needed to say. Lake knew she was busted.

But that didn't mean she was ready to admit it.

"Wh… what are you talking about, Aspen? How dare you? I don't *steal* designs—"

Teague pumped his fist in the air, and the other guys high-fived over my head.

"Lake, let me save you the effort. You know the laptop you left here? Well, it wasn't hard to get past the password. I saw your emails about my work."

"I… I don't understand. What were you doing in my email? Were you snooping? You know that's grounds for termination, Aspen—"

"Don't worry about it, Lake. I quit."

I hung up the phone, a combination of abject terror and triumph running through me at the same time. The sensation was so strong I ran over to the kitchen sink in case I got sick.

But I didn't.

The guys didn't share my trepidation. "Fuck yeah!" Luke said, clapping his hands.

"Oh my god, oh my god, oh my god," I said, splashing cool water on my face. "What the hell did I just do?"

Luke walked over to me and placed both his hands on my shoulders. "Aspen, you just did what's known as kicking ass and taking names. You are officially a badass."

I looked up at him, not entirely sure I agreed. "Holy shit. I have rent to cover and a student loan to pay back." I needed a new cell phone, too.

"Okay. Okay. You're freaking. That's normal. But we can help. As soon as the car's ready, we'll head back to Manhattan, following you in one of our cars. We'll load up all your stuff, and bring you back. Teague's grandparents have a guest cottage you can stay in."

I looked down at my feet, confused by the fluttering in my chest. What he was saying made no sense at all. But it was starting to.

"I can't leave my roommate high and dry," I started to say.

Teague took my hand. "Look. I'll loan you the money to pay rent until she gets someone new. And you'll be living at my grandparents for free, anyway."

I shook my head. "No. No. That's crazy. I'll head back to Manhattan and get another job."

Yeah right. After I'd pissed off Lake LaRenne, my name would be mud in the industry.

"Aspen," Luke said gently, "you can get a job here for the summer. Remember, we know everyone. And then you can head to LA with us."

It was too much. All too much. I grabbed a seat at the dining table and put my head in my hands.

The guys said nothing, which I appreciated. They knew I needed a moment to think.

I could come up with a dozen reasons why Teague, Luke, and Brant were crazy for suggesting something I had no business going along with.

But I could think of three good reasons why I should.

I looked up, tired of being afraid.

"Fuck it, guys. Let's do it."

Holy shit. Did I really just say that?

But I must have, as evidenced by all the hooting and hollering I was surrounded by.

"Last one in the pool buys dinner!" I screamed, running out the back door while tearing off my clothes.

With three hot guys in tow, who'd just extended me the invitation of a lifetime.

I didn't know how I would manage things, or what I would tell my parents, but I knew that with these guys by my side, shit would work out.

Like it always did for them, and was beginning to, for me, as well.

Did you enjoy Lexi's story in Dripping Wet?
Check out the other sexy, steamy stories in the
Filthy, Dirty Summer Series

and... find all Mika Lane books here

GET A FREE SHORT STORY
Join my Insider Group

ABOUT THE AUTHOR

I'm contemporary romance author Mika Lane, and am all about bringing you sexy, sassy stories with imperfect heroines and the bad-a*s dudes they bring to their knees. And I have a special love for romance with multiple guys because why should we have to settle for just one hunky man?

Please join my Insider Group and be the first to hear about giveaways, sales, pre-orders, ARCs, and most importantly, a free sexy short story: http://mikalane. com/join-mailing-list/.

Writing has been a passion of mine since, well, forever (my first book was "The Day I Ate the Milky-way," a true fourth-grade masterpiece). These days, steamy romance, both dark and funny, gives purpose to my days and nights as I create worlds and characters who defy the imagination. I live in magical Northern California with my own handsome alpha dude, sometimes known as Mr. Mika Lane, and two devilish cats named Chuck and Murray. These three males also defy my imagination from time to time.

A lover of shiny things, I've been known to try new recipes on unsuspecting friends, find hiding places so I can read undisturbed, and spend my last dollar on a plane ticket somewhere.

Check out my latest series, The Men at Work Collection, about hot men and the professions that make them successful masters of the universe... and the women they love.

I'll always promise you a hot, sexy romp with kick-ass but imperfect heroines, and some version of a modern-day happily ever after.

I LOVE to hear from readers when I'm not dreaming up naughty tales to share. Join my Insider Group so we can get to know each other better http://mikalane.com/join-mailing-list, or contact me here: https://mikalane.com/contact.

Printed in Great Britain
by Amazon